The Christmas Proposal

CHERYL WRIGHT

THE CHRISTMAS PROPOSAL

Copyright 2018 by Cheryl Wright

Cover Artist: Black Widow Books

Dedication

To Margaret Tanner, my very dear friend and fellow author, for her enduring encouragement and friendship.

To Alan, my husband of over forty-six years, who has been a relentless supporter of my writing and dreams for many years.

To Virginia McKevitt, cover artist and friend, who always creates the most amazing covers for my books.

To You, my wonderful readers, who encourage me to continue writing these stories. It is such a joy knowing so many of you enjoy reading my stories as much as I love writing them for you.

Table of Contents

Chapter One

Mandy Scott stood at the window staring at the covering of snow. It was pure white for as far as the eye could see.

She loved this time of year in Winston Montana with its snow-covered peaks and tree branches heavy with snow. She loved watching children throw snowballs at each other and toboggan down the slopes of the streets surrounding her little cottage.

Wrapping her arms around herself she sighed.

She loved it except that every year around this time she faced the same dilemma. Every year at this time she beat herself up about not having a significant other in her life.

Her sisters had all married, and her brother was engaged to a wonderful woman. She was the only one *left on the shelf* as they all laughingly called it.

Only it wasn't funny. Not really.

Mandy didn't see it as a joke. It stung every time someone made a comment about her relationship status. Or should she say *non-relationship* status?

At nearly thirty years old, everyone thought it was time.

Except Mandy.

She was happy with her life exactly the way it was. She loved her career as senior reporter at News of the Day and had no intention of leaving it any time soon.

The pressure she was put under leading up to the holidays each year was suffocating her.

Maybe she wouldn't go this year. That would solve all her problems.

Her parents put on a huge family party leading up to the holidays each year. Everyone attended. Everyone with their partners and their offspring, that is.

Then there was Mandy.

She had tried repeatedly to get out of going, but her mother always insisted. She'd even tried to use work as an excuse.

Her mother saw right through her excuses and demanded she go. For her own good of course.

She turned away from the scene in front of her. Suddenly she couldn't bear to watch the happy couples hand-in-hand, frolicking through the snow.

As much as she was happy with her life, sometimes it would be nice to have that special someone to love.

It was early November, and already she was worrying about the holidays.

* * *

Mandy tied her hair back in a ponytail, then pulled the apron around herself and prepared to help her mother with the holiday baking.

She had fond memories of standing in this very kitchen, helping her mother prepare for the upcoming celebrations.

They baked rum balls, biscuits, Christmas puddings and cakes, as well as traditional shortbread. There were weeks of baking with many of the items being bundled up to give as gifts, with the majority going to elderly friends who were no longer able to bake their own.

"Well, don't just stand there!" Helena Scott told her daughter. "There is so much to do in the next few weeks." There was nothing like being prepared.

Mandy instinctively knew what was coming next. "Who are you bringing to the family celebrations this year?" Her mother meant no harm, but it pulled at her heart strings every year to have to say the same thing.

Mandy adjusted her apron, tied it a little tighter. "I haven't decided yet." The words were out before she could stop them.

"How wonderful!" Helena exclaimed.

From the look on her face, Mandy knew she had to come through now. What had she done? She couldn't just dream a man out of thin air.

"Why have you kept him secret," her mother wanted to know. "What is his name, how old is he, when and where did you meet him, why haven't you…."

"Seriously, Mother!"

The room went quiet. "I'm sorry, darling," she said. "But this is so exciting."

Mandy rummaged through her mother's recipe books, pretending to try and decide what she would cook. "Rum balls look good," she said more brightly than she felt.

Now all she had to do was find her perfect date. It wouldn't be long, and her entire family would hear she was finally bringing a man to the celebrations.

* * *

Noah Gleeson stared at the mess around him.

Winston Montana was a long way from his home-town of Buckeye Arizona.

There was nothing left for him there, and when the opportunity for a transfer had presented itself, he grabbed it with both hands.

When he found out he'd be moving house less than two months before Christmas, he hesitated. Who wouldn't?

His hesitation didn't last long. Forty seconds, if that. With no family to consider, he'd decided to take the chance. Now, as he stood in his new kitchen surrounded by boxes, he wasn't so sure. But it was too late to back out now.

The moving company people had left less than an hour ago, and now Noah felt lost.

He'd bought this house sight unseen. A massive leap of faith on his part. Something he'd never done before with such a big purchase. But time was of the essence; he didn't have time to fly to Montana and check out houses, and so he'd contacted an estate agent who had been recommended, and the rest was history.

He was more than happy with his purchase, and the agent had gone the extra mile. He arrived to find a bottle of champagne on the table, along with a box of chocolates.

He needed a strong coffee just thinking about it, but he had no idea where to find a coffee mug, let alone the coffee.

It seemed the perfect time to familiarize himself with his new home town.

As he wandered around the small town, the change of lifestyle hit him square in the face. He'd lived in Buckeye for most of his life and had enjoyed the city life, with all its restaurants, bars, and active nightlife.

Sure, there were stores. A café, dress shop, hairdresser and a few other stores, but it was not like anything he was used to. Noah was certain Winston would shut down around eight every night.

He had planned to eat out tonight, so he'd better get there early or risk missing out.

He came to a halt outside the quaint little café, contemplating whether or not to go in. He stared at the flashing holiday lights, daring him to ignore the upcoming celebrations.

He gingerly opened the door and forced his face into the mask he used to stop people wanting to know him.

* * *

"And this is Noah Gleeson, your new boss."

Mandy glanced up from her desk and eyed her new boss. She knew he was coming. Heck, she'd even applied for the position.

As one of the senior journalists at News of the Day, she thought she was a certainty to get it, but it wasn't to be. The company already had someone picked out at head office.

She tried not to let it get to her. After all, they had to work together.

"Pleased to meet you, Mr Gleeson," she said, swallowing back her pride, and extending her hand as she stood.

He smiled pleasantly beneath the mask, but Mandy could see right through him. He was going through the motions. She put it down to new job, new town.

"Noah, please," he said abruptly. "Mr Gleeson is," He stopped suddenly and swallowed. "was my dad."

"Oh." Mandy loved both her parents and couldn't bare to lose them. It was quite apparent he'd lost his dad. And fairly recently if she was any judge of character. "I'm sorry."

How terribly sad. But he brushed her words away with a flick of his hand.

He wasn't very old either. Maybe just a few years older than her?

Not that Mandy was interested in anything about Noah, except his work ethic. She distanced herself from most of her colleagues.

She enjoyed her privacy, as much as you could have in a small town like Winston, so she rarely fraternized with her work mates. Especially Harry Simpson. Even now she could feel his eyes burn a hole in her back.

"We'll get together soon, once I've settled in," he said.

She frowned. *Get together? What was that about?*

"So I can see where you're up to with your current assignments."

She nodded. Of course he'd need to know where she was at. It was his job.

The job she wanted.

She shook her self mentally. It was not Noah's fault she didn't get the job. She just had to move on and get on with it.

"My door is always open," he said, as he began to walk away.

She nodded but was convinced she wouldn't be spending much time with Noah Gleeson. Not if she could help it.

* * *

Mandy sat in the staff lunchroom nibbling on a sandwich. It had been a long day and it wasn't even half over yet.

She was working on a big assignment. Big for Winston anyway. One day she would break out of the small-town reporter persona she carried everywhere she went.

Her goal was to work in one of the big cities. Report on the important stuff. Investigative reporter, that was her dream job. Getting into the nitty-gritty of the latest political scandal or finding the killer on a cold case.

Instead she was writing about the Jones's 50th Wedding Anniversary and the Winston Cattery that needed more people to adopt.

In her heart, Mandy knew she would never leave this quaint little town. Her family were here – her tribe – and she would never abandon them.

She picked up her mug of coffee and was bringing it to her lips when she felt someone behind her. she spun around, spilling her coffee as she did.

"Heck!" It was everywhere. All over the table and threatening to spill onto her clothes.

Noah was there in a flash. "I'm sorry if I startled you," he said, reaching for a towel. "Let me clean up this mess."

They reached for the mug at the same time and their fingers brushed. He looked up suddenly. At the same time, she felt a buzz run through her.

"I, uh, thanks," she said, backing off. He had it under control.

"Any suggestions of where I could eat in this town?" The question came out of the blue. It was the last thing she expected him to say.

"The café?"

He nodded. "Yeah, been there a couple of times already. Thought there might be somewhere else."

"In Winston?" She laughed.

He smiled at her, and she felt her resolve melting.

"You could have dinner at my place tonight." The words were out before she could stop them. She bit her lip. Why on earth did she invite him to dinner?

Perhaps because he was new in town? Or maybe she was feeling a little vulnerable right now? *She was not lonely!*

Besides, it was only a friendly dinner welcoming a new colleague. Of her place of employment. She was being kind.

He frowned. "You don't have to," he said apologetically. "Please don't feel obligated."

"No. It's fine," she said. Was she trying to convince herself or Noah. "Is there anything you can't or don't eat?" Now she was sounding like her mother.

He rubbed his belly. "Cast iron stomach. I can handle pretty much anything you throw at me." He smiled. She liked it when he genuinely smiled, instead of the mask he seemed to wear most of the time.

"Then it's settled. Six o'clock, my place."

She spent the rest of the afternoon working out a dinner menu in her head as she worked on the local Sheriff's Office turning one hundred.

It was a beautiful old building, and she'd had the pleasure of a full tour, as well as interviewing the Sheriff and some of his more senior staff.

The two-page spread was due to be published in two days, in time for the celebrations, so she'd better get on with it.

Steak, baked potatoes, beans.

That sounded like a perfect meal for a man far from home. It also sounded a little cliché but heck, she was sure he'd like it.

What man didn't like a steak and three veg meal? Okay, two veg, but that was beside the point.

She sat tapping her pen on the desk as she thought.

"A penny for them."

She looked up to see Noah standing in front of her.

"Huh?"

"You looked deep in thought." He stood staring down at her. "I wanted to check if I can bring anything tonight."

"Tonight?" She shook herself. Her brain wasn't working, she'd been so deep in her work.

"Dinner. Look, if you've changed your mind…"

She abruptly stood. "Of course not, I was just distracted is all." She breathed in and the aroma of his cologne as it invaded her nostrils. "I, um," she was unexpectedly tongue-tied.

He stood watching her. Waiting for her to get the words out.

Suddenly the words were rushing out of her mouth. "I thought we'd have steak. Is that okay?"

He rubbed his hands together. "I can't remember the last time I had steak. It sounds wonderful."

"Steak it is then." She began to sit again. "I have to get back to this, sorry. I have a tight deadline." She smiled gingerly and he turned to walk away but turned back again.

"You'd better give me your address." She scribbled it on a piece of paper and handed it to him. Their fingers brushed, and she felt that tingle of a thrill again.

This absolutely wouldn't do. And now she was having him to dinner.

Her mother would be ecstatic.

Chapter Two

What was he thinking? Accepting an invitation for dinner from a work colleague he'd just met.

Crazy.

Not only did it go against his work ethics, it left him vulnerable. Especially since he was feeling things about Mandy he had no right to feel.

Noah reminded himself tonight's dinner was nothing more than the chance to have a good homecooked meal, along with some much-needed company.

These past months had been lonely. And sad.

Losing both his parents at the same time due to an horrific car crash was beyond comprehension. And it wasn't as though he had someone to share his grief with. As an only child, he alone endured the heartache of becoming an orphan in his twenties.

Noah sat back in his office chair and rubbed his hand across his chin. Bristles were beginning to push through. That wouldn't do.

Mandy had been kind enough to offer him dinner; the least he could do was turn up looking presentable.

And, oh my, he couldn't go there empty handed.

He had to clean up *and* find somewhere to buy a bottle of wine.

He stared at his watch. 5.15pm. He only had forty-five minutes to shower and change *and* get the wine. For once he was pleased his new house was walking distance from the office. Mandy's wasn't that far away either.

He stood and stared out across the empty office.

It was turning out to be a good move. Despite the lack of night life, everything here seemed a bit more relaxed.

Working sixty plus hours a week had taken its toll. The death of his parents had put more stress on him than he'd first realized. The regret of not spending enough time with them over the years had washed over him like a black cloud. A cloud that refused to dissipate, no matter what.

When the chance of a transfer came up, he jumped at it. Especially since his doctor had stressed he was working his way into an early grave and had to find a way to change his lifestyle.

A new start. That's what he decided he'd needed. Get away from the memories of what might have been and start afresh.

That's exactly what he'd done, and now here he was in Winston Montana. In the middle of the snow season.

He was so not used to this sort of weather. It was almost unheard of in Buckeye.

He mentally shook himself. There was no time for reminiscing. *Get out of the office and get ready.*

Noah took a deep breath and forced himself to move one foot after the other. What the hell had he been thinking accepting a dinner invitation from a total stranger?

What's done is done, he decided, and moved toward the front door. The cleaners had already arrived, so at least he didn't have to remember the security codes tonight.

He pulled on his coat and pulled his collar up to protect his neck. Stepping outside, he finally realized why he'd been hesitant to leave the office.

It was like stepping into a cold storage unit out there. At least the thick gloves helped protect his hands from the freezing temperatures. *What was he thinking coming to this snow-ridden town?*

Still, a white Christmas would be a nice change. It was a pity he'd have to spend it alone.

As he walked briskly toward his new home, a snowball hit him square in the face, almost toppling him. He glanced up, annoyed.

"Sorry Mister," a kid yelled and ran the other way.

Noah brushed himself off and continued his walk. "Damned kids," he muttered to himself as he continued the short walk home.

It was turning out to be a long day. He wondered what the evening would bring.

* * *

Mandy hadn't been this nervous about a date since she was a teenager.

But it wasn't a date, and she needed to remind herself of that fact. This was her being kind to a colleague who was new in town.

Breathe. Just breathe.

She was getting herself worked up about nothing. Noah seemed like a nice guy and had been thrown in the deep end. From what she'd been told, he'd only been given a few weeks get himself organized to move here.

Alfred Kingston, Mandy's previous boss, had suffered a heart attack at work. It had not only traumatized the staff but left a gap in management when he decided to retire early.

She was certain she would get the job, but so did the half dozen other people who also applied. In the end, it went to an outsider. Noah Gleeson.

He was senior management at head office, so it made sense.

She was sure there was a story behind him moving from the big city to here, but it was none of her business.

She glanced up at the clock as she put the finishing touches on the table settings. Ten minutes before he arrived.

She'd pulled out her best china for tonight's dinner, and her favorite tablecloth.

Her mother would be proud.

Mandy bustled around, preparing for her dinner guest. She became more and more nervous as time went on. But why?

Perhaps she was unconsciously trying to make a good impression on her new boss.

As she shuffled past the hallway mirror she stopped momentarily and checked herself out. Urgh! What an almighty mess!

She snatched another glance at her watch. He would be here any moment now!

Mandy ran to the bedroom, with a view to changing into fresh clothes. She was rifling through her clothes when the doorbell rang.

Her heartbeat ratched up, and she began to panic. What on earth would he think of her, hosting him for dinner wearing her work clothes?

She sat on the edge of the bed and took a few deep breaths.

Can't do a thing about it. Might as well suck it up.

With her resolve melting away, Mandy quickly ran a brush through her wild hair, then went to the front door. She took another few calming breaths before opening it.

An artic breeze swept through the door, and she shivered. "Come in out of that freezing cold air!" she said, grabbing his sleeve and pulling Noah inside.

He shoved a bottle of wine into her hands, then brushed his shoes on the door mat before stepping inside. "It is rather cold," he said. "I'm not used to this weather."

The moment he was inside, she slammed the door, as though blocking the world away from them.

She looked him up and down. "You'll have to replace that," she said, pointing to his inadequate coat. "You'll soon find out a trench coat doesn't cut it out here." She smiled, but realized it probably looked as though she was mocking him.

He laughed. "Too late. I've already found out!" She helped him out of his flimsy coat and hung it on the rack near the door.

"You'll need a thick pullover too. At least you've got the gloves right."

She moved toward the living room, motioning for him to follow. "I have a fire going. Come in and warm up." After the cool air pushing its way through the cottage, the warmth of the fire would be more than a little welcomed.

"This is lovely," he said, glancing around. "My place is way too big for one person."

She arched an eyebrow at him. "It's a long story," he said. "Maybe one day I'll tell you about it."

Mandy motioned for him to sit by the fire. One of the first things she'd done when she'd brought the cottage was ensure the armchairs were close to the fire. She was certain they'd be needed in the winter, and she was right.

He stood, uncertain of where to sit. "Please, anywhere is fine. Warm up, you look frozen to the bone."

"You're not wrong, Mandy," he said tentatively. "I appreciate your invitation for dinner. I promise not to infringe on your kindness in the future." He looked to the ground, and she wondered why he felt so self conscious about it.

"Honestly, Noah, it's fine. I much prefer to cook for two than one."

He took his place near the fire and began to warm his hands. She sat opposite him, not saying a word. It felt a little awkward.

"Is that,"

Mandy listened. "Yeah, the baked potatoes are almost ready. Wine before dinner?"

"I'll follow your lead," he said, and stood up. "What can I do to help?"

She stiffened. "You're my guest," she said, taken aback that he'd even offered.

He arched an eyebrow at her.

She shrugged. "But if that's what rocks your boat."

He followed her to the tiny kitchen which was off the living room. "Smells amazing," he told her as he ducked his head to avoid hitting it on the door frame.

She pulled two steaks out of the refrigerator and turned to him. "How do you have your steak?"

She had the pan heating up and once ready, placed both steaks on the heat, searing them.

"Medium rare. Shall I open the wine?"

Mandy reached into an overhead cupboard to retrieve two wine glasses, but they were a little out of reach.

"Let me." He leaned across her, brushing her shoulder. Warmth ran through her body. It was at that point she knew she was in trouble.

She watched as he poured the wine, taking the half full bottle to the table, and placing the two full glasses in front of each setting.

Mandy busied herself with the steaks, then grabbed two plates out of the cupboard. She drained the green beans, added a steak to each plate, then last of all, took the baked potatoes out of the oven.

"It looks and smells amazing, Mandy," Noah said genuinely. "I haven't eaten this well in months."

She laughed. "You haven't tried it yet. It might be horrible."

Noah frowned at her. "I hope you're joking," he said. "You have been so kind to me, inviting me here tonight. I'm a complete stranger, and yet…" He indicated the table and all its contents. "You put on a wonderful spread like this. You have no idea how much this means to me."

Mandy was taken aback. His words were heartfelt, she could tell. Head office had told them nothing of their new boss except he was available to be there quickly.

She stared at him for several moments. "You are very welcome," she said. "But honestly, I'm not the best cook, so I really hope it's okay."

She sat down, and he followed suit. He took a sip of his wine and lifted his knife and fork. He cut through the steak. "Perfect," he said, taking a mouthful. "Absolute perfection."

Mandy watched him for a few moments as he ate. He seemed to savor it. She wondered how long it had been since he'd eaten a home cooked meal.

"How long have you worked for News of the Day?" she suddenly asked, trying to break the awkward silence.

He looked up from his food. "About ten years. Worked my way up the ranks," he said.

"Me too," she said. "I guess we have that in common. Just so you know," she said, wondering if it was the right thing to do. "I applied for your job."

He nodded. "I know," he said. "I'm sorry."

What was he sorry for? That he was the best person for the job? Or that he thought he'd upset her by being awarded the position she had coveted for some time?

"Don't be," she said quickly. "I only told you in case someone else did."

He finished the last bite of food and stood, walking toward the sink. "I'll do that." She reached for his plate, but instead brushed his hand.

She stared into his eyes. "I," Words eluded her. She'd never had a reaction like this before – to any man.

Ever.

She certainly didn't want to feel this way about her boss. Oh my gosh. She was falling for her boss!

"Mandy, I," He finished rinsing his plate, then reached for her hands. His were warm and felt comforting.

He stepped closer. Her treacherous body moved closer to him, and he reached around to pull her close.

She rested her head against his chest. Suddenly her head snapped up and she stepped out of his embrace. "I, we can't do this!"

She turned and busied herself with dessert – lemon meringue pie with double cream.

"You are a seriously good cook," he said, totally ignoring the fact they'd been embracing each other just moments ago.

Mandy sliced the pie and dished some out for each of them. She carried it to the table, and Noah carried the cream.

"This is delicious," he announced after the first mouthful. "Where did you learn to cook like this?" He stared into her face. "And don't tell me you bought it. This is far from a bought pie."

"I bought it," she said blandly.

He stared at her for about five seconds then a slow smile crossed his face. "No, you didn't."

She grinned. "No, I didn't. I made it. Yesterday actually. Perfect timing."

They returned to the living room when dinner was over. "Mandy, you have no idea what tonight has meant to me," he said, avoiding the fact they'd embraced. They'd made a silent pact not to mention it again. Two lonely people connecting on a higher level.

"You are welcome to come again sometime," Mandy said. He was good company. But on second thought, tongues might start wagging at work.

"Thank you, I appreciate it." He stared at the fire for a few minutes before speaking again. "I'm not sure it's such a good idea though. Especially given..."

She nodded, knowing he was alluding to their earlier encounter. "I understand," she whispered as he stood to leave.

"I should go before this snow gets too heavy."

Mandy followed him to the front door. "Do you have far to go?"

He pulled on his coat and gloves. "I'm about ten minutes away by foot. Maybe twenty in this weather."

"Promise me you'll buy more appropriate clothing."

"I promise," he said. "Thank you for a wonderful night," He leaned forward and kissed Mandy lightly on the cheek, then turned to walk away.

"You're walking?" she called after him. "In this weather?"

He turned back to stare at her. "I'll be fine," he promised.

"But still, let me drive you." He was so not used to Montana weather, that much was clear.

"Thanks for the offer, but I'll be perfectly fine." He gave her a wave and was on his way.

She closed the door then leaned against it, touching her cheek where she could still feel his kiss.

Chapter Three

Noah tossed and turned in bed that night, any sort of decent sleep alluding him.

He had met the most wonderful woman, and she was out of reach. Why did it always happen this way?

He had a strong work ethic, and that included not fraternizing with his staff. It did him a lot of good in this case.

Not.

He'd accepted an innocent dinner invitation, but instead of just filling his belly, it sent his hormones every which way.

That hadn't happened to him since Abigail.

He'd thought he was in love with her, and she'd said she loved him. But deep down, he hadn't ever believed she did. Not really.

Not in that heart-fluttering way he thought soul-mates should feel for each other.

He'd never had a thrill from touching her. He did with Mandy.

He'd never felt tingles in his hands from brushing up against her. He did with Mandy.

And he'd never felt a warmth that invaded his entire body like he did with Mandy.

Oh man. He had it bad. And he'd only known her for a day; what would it be like after a month or two?

Noah ducked his head in under the covers. He did not want to go to work. He'd been there one whole day and already he wanted to disappear.

And all because of Mandy.

She'd felt so good when he held her in his arms. She didn't seem too upset about being close to him either. At least in the beginning.

But they were both lonely. He'd concluded that on the cold walk back home. There was nothing like an icy cold breeze and a face full of snow to bring you to your senses.

So why had he tossed and turned all night?

He glanced across at the clock. It was way to early to get up and was still dark outside. He dragged himself out of bed and wrapped the comforter around himself in an effort to keep warm.

It wasn't very successful.

Noah pushed the curtains aside and stared out across the horizon. He could see the sun trying to peak out over the mountains. He'd never witnessed such beauty in Buckeye.

He listened carefully but couldn't hear anything. At. All.

He'd only been here a few days, but already he was noticing changes. The hustle and bustle of the city was gone, and so were his stress levels.

The peacefulness of Winston was amazing. As he made his way toward the bathroom, he could hear the beginnings of birds twittering.

He'd never noticed that in the city.

The occasional car drove down his street. Back home there would have been dozens, if not hundreds, in the same amount of time.

He started to whistle as he turned on the faucets for the shower. He pulled himself up. What was that about?

As he stepped into the shower cubicle, he realized it had already started.

His new life.

And he was really happy about it.

* * *

Mandy looked up from her computer as Noah came through the door.

He strolled over to her desk. "Good morning," he said. "Thanks again for last night."

Heads shot up around them, curiosity written all over the faces of the other staff.

She was right – tongues would be wagging, and Noah had just put plenty of fuel on the fire.

"Dinner was delicious," he said. "I really do appreciate it. I hadn't had a home-cooked meal for several months," he told her as he fingered the papers on her desk.

"Really?" What a sad situation when a man had to eat out all the time. "Maybe we can do it again sometime." Mandy felt like pinching herself.

One night with Noah was near torture. Not because she didn't like him, because that certainly wasn't the case.

No, the problem was in the fact she did like him – way too much for her own good.

"Perhaps you can come to my place next time." She nodded tentatively. Not sure it was such a good idea to go to her boss's place, any more than it was for him to go to hers.

At least this way it was non-committal.

"Great," he said enthusiastically, totally misinterpreting her response. "How does Saturday week sound?"

He must have noted her confusion. Saturday week was a long way off. "I need time to sort out the moving mess. If that's okay," he added quickly.

She shrugged, then her eyes slid sideways. Their work colleagues were hanging on every word. "I'll walk with you to your office," Mandy said, grabbing some files off her desk. "I need to discuss this assignment with you."

He frowned, obviously not understanding her intent, until her eyes slid sideways once more.

"Oh sure," he said, and strolled casually toward his office.

He turned on his computer as he sat behind the big redwood desk that once belonged to Alfred

Kingston. He looked quite regal sitting there in his padded leather chair.

He leaned back and put his hands behind his head, in exactly the same way Mr Kingston had done for many years.

This helped. It really helped.

It put things into more perspective. Suddenly she could see Noah as her boss. As her Mr Kingston instead of Noah. Sounded stupid when she thought about it, but it just might help her dilemma.

"What did you want to discuss?" he asked innocently. "An assignment did you say?"

His secretary strolled into the office. "Sorry Mr Gleeson, but I need these purchase orders approved immediately."

Mandy held the folders close to her chest and stared at him. That was exactly what she needed – a distraction.

"Mandy, I…"

"It's fine. I'll talk to you later." Right at that moment, Mandy had no intention of doing any such thing.

* * *

"So who is he?" Her mother asked the question innocently enough. Or so it seemed, but Mandy knew better.

Her mother was always probing, needing to know if she'd hooked up with any eligible young men of late. Not that there were many eligible men in Winston. Which often seemed like a good thing.

No, it was only the blow-ins – like Noah – that were available.

Mandy knew she was a disappointment to her mother in the marrying stakes. Her sisters Jenny and Allison were married, but no children yet, and her brother Thomas was engaged to be married.

Helena saw it her duty as a mother to see her daughter married and happy with children running at her feet.

And if it didn't happen in the next year or so, according to her mother, Mandy would be a spinster for the rest of her life.

She groaned inwardly.

"Who is who?" She had no idea what Helena was on about.

"A friend drove past your place last night, and a very tall, very handsome young man was entering your cottage.

Mandy's eyes opened in surprise. "Last night? Who did you send Mother?" She put her hands on her hips, her temper barely under control.

"Send? Oh no," Helena said quietly. "You have it all wrong. A friend happened…"

Her brain started to tick over. "Were you spying on me, Mother? The fact your friend was there at that precise moment…"

Helena wiped her hands on her apron. "I heard a whisper you'd be *entertaining* a young man." She said the words as though that would justify spying on her.

As much as she loved living here in Winston, she also hated the way the grapevine worked.

"Really, Mother!" Exasperation would be an understatement when it came to Helena's efforts to match her up. The end game being marrying her off in the quickest possible time.

"Neither of us are interested in dating, or getting married, or anything else." She faced her mother square on, hands on hips.

From the look on Helena's face, she wasn't buying it.

"We only met a week or so ago for goodness sake." She picked up her coffee and walked briskly into the living room, snuggling up to the roaring fire.

"Who's this young man I keep hearing about," her father asked. Mandy was ready to flee but knew her parents had her best interests at heart.

"He's my boss, and we're *not* dating." It was a conspiracy, she was certain of it.

"Bring him around Saturday night so we can meet him." Her parents were relentless.

She braced herself for the backlash. "We already have plans for that night. And before you say anything," she said, teeth gritted, "It is just dinner, it is *not* a date!"

She practically ran into the kitchen, dumped her cup in the sink, and headed to the back door. "Goodbye, Mother. I have to run."

She couldn't get out of there quick enough.

* * *

"Are we still on for Saturday night?"

It was an innocent enough question, and at least this time Noah had asked away from the flapping ears of the office staff.

Mandy continued to eat her sandwich as he slipped into the chair opposite her, waiting for a response. She covered her mouth with her hand. "Uh,"

"Great! I'm looking forward to it." He began to stand again.

"Noah," she said. "I…"

"Oh, I didn't give you a time, did I?" He thought for a moment. "Is seven o'clock okay?" He didn't wait for an answer, but instead got up and strolled out of the room, whistling.

Mandy groaned. They were already the talk of the office. And her parents. Not to mention the grapevine of Winston.

She leaned forward and banged her head gently on the lunch table.

She had royally dumped herself in this position but wasn't convinced she would have it any other way.

Noah was great company, she was lonely, he probably was too, and they both enjoyed a good home cooked meal. *What was wrong with that?*

Except the fact he was her boss, and the whole town was talking about them.

Mandy shoved her chair back and cringed as it scraped along the floor. She jumped as she felt a hand on her shoulder.

Her head spun around, expecting to find Noah there, but instead she found herself face to face with Horrible Harry, a sneer on his face.

Horrible Harry, as she'd named him was one of her *colleagues.* He'd harassed her from the day he'd arrived some months earlier.

"Get your hands off me, Harry!" She stood and shook herself out of his grip.

Instead of taking the hint, Harry moved closer – he was trying to kiss her! Yuk.

She raised her voice and stepped back. "Get away from me!"

"What's going on here?" Noah was there in a flash. His office was not far away, and he must have heard the altercation.

"Nothing. Everything is alright," Harry protested.

Noah looked to Mandy. "Everything is *not* alright," she said. "Harry is… He has…" She couldn't get the words out, so she stopped talking.

Noah frowned. "Mr Simpson," he said. "Wait for me in my office."

After the other man had left, he turned to Mandy. "He has been what, Mandy? I need to know so I can deal with this."

She looked to the ground and spoke quietly. "He's been harassing me since he came to work here a few months ago. Touching me, trying to kiss me…" She fought back tears. *She was not going to crumble in front of Noah.* "I've considered leaving, but I love my job."

He pulled out a chair and indicated for her to sit. Then he made her a fresh coffee. "*You* are not leaving. You're my best reporter." His words warmed her. "And besides, why should you leave because of someone else's bad behavior? Stay here until I come and get you. Is that alright?" He put the mug of coffee in front of her. "Simpson and I are going to have a chat."

"I don't want…"

"His behavior is not okay, Mandy." He turned and walked out of the room, leaving her to drink her coffee, and contemplate why she'd ever put up with Harry's unwanted advances.

After all, no means no, but Harry wouldn't listen.

* * *

"Consider this your first and last warning, Mr Simpson." Harry sat across the desk from Noah looking glum. "I will not tolerate this sort of behavior, and if it happens again – to any of the women in the office – you will be immediately terminated. If I could do it right now, legally, I would."

Harry glared at him.

"Do you understand me?" He kept his voice quiet and was barely under control.

Harry sat up straighter and barked out the words. "It's only because she's your girlfriend. Otherwise you wouldn't care."

Noah took a deep breath. This wasn't happening. Only two weeks into his new job and he was dealing with idiots.

"Number one, Mandy is *not* my girlfriend – not that it's your business. Number two, it wouldn't matter who you'd targeted, the outcome would be the same. I will *not* allow women to be harassed. Understand? Now get out of my office!"

His temper was barely under control by this stage. *The gall of the man!*

"Mr Simpson," he called after the man's retreating back. "Go home and think about what you've done. I don't want to see you again today."

"What about my assignments?" Harry asked.

Noah sighed. "Come in at six tomorrow and catch up. Otherwise I'll be docking your pay."

Harry began to protest but thought better of it and quickly left.

Noah leaned back in his chair trying to calm himself down. He still had to deal with Mandy, make sure she was okay.

He stormed into the lunch room. "He's gone," Noah told her, taking the chair opposite.

She looked up sharply. "You didn't sack him? Tell me you didn't sack him!"

He frowned. It's what the mongrel deserved. "No, I didn't. But he's on notice. If it happens again…" He clenched his teeth at the thought.

"I'll tell you, I promise."

He slid his hand across the table to cover hers. "I couldn't bear for anything to happen to you, Mandy," he said quietly.

She nodded, and he pulled his hand away, realizing perhaps he had overstepped the mark.

"My mother thinks we're an item," she said suddenly.

He laughed out loud.

"It's not funny," Mandy said, obviously annoyed. "She heard a whisper," she rolled her eyes as if to say, *Winston grapevine.* "She got someone to drive past. They saw you go into my place."

He sat quietly and listened. She obviously needed to talk.

"To top it off, Father invited us to dinner next Saturday night." She pulled a face. "He wants to meet you."

His heart started beating faster. "But *we're* having dinner Saturday night."

He looked at her eagerly. Too eagerly perhaps.

"I know. I told him. It only added fuel to the fire. Because having dinner means going on a date." She pouted.

"Luckily I haven't mentioned our numerous lunch *dates*. They'd really go to town. My family interfere to the point of distraction sometimes." He could see she was annoyed and wanted to make it right. Especially after the Harry incident.

He stood abruptly and grabbed her hand. "Come on," he said. "We're going for coffee. You're obviously stressed, so we need to leave the office for awhile."

She glanced down at their entwined hands. He quickly let go. "Sorry," he said. "I presumed too much."

Mandy shook her head. "No, it's okay. It feels good." She hooked her hand in his again and they strolled out of the office, not caring who saw.

Chapter Four

"Two cappuccinos, and…." He turned to Mandy. "Choose a cake or muffin or something."

She shook her head. "I'm fine, really."

He insisted, pointing to the display cabinet. "I'm starving, and don't want to eat alone. Pick one."

They did look rather yummy, so she gave in and chose baked cheesecake with cherries.

"Cream on the side," he added.

Ah well, it didn't happen often.

After paying, he guided her to a table in the corner, where they'd have more privacy. "Do you want to talk about Harry?"

She shook her head again. He'd been the bane of her life since he'd arrived, but it looked like Noah was going to sort him out.

"About your parents," he began, and she winced.

"They're being painful. But it's nothing new. They think I should be married with 3.5 kids by now." She pulled a face, and Noah laughed. "Mother says if I don't marry in the next two years, I'll be a spinster forever." She laughed and felt better for it.

He reached across the table and covered her hand with his. He quickly pulled it back when their order arrived.

"Thanks Sherry," Mandy said as the waitress left them.

She turned back to Noah. "I wish they'd get off my back." Her shoulders slumped.

His slow burning smile caught her attention. "What if you had a boyfriend? Would they leave you alone then?" He reached across the table again and squeezed her hand.

"Probably," she answered cautiously. "What are you up to?"

"Take up their offer," he said. "We can have dinner some other time. I want to take the pressure off you. I know the Harry situation hasn't helped either."

She wondered if he had an ulterior motive, but in the little time she'd known Noah, he'd been nothing but honest and upfront with her.

"We enjoy each other's company," he said. "I love your cooking, you're yet to try mine, but I think my cooking is passable." He grinned at her. "Maybe."

She wasn't sure what to think. Could she risk getting too close? Especially with her alarmingly handsome boss, who just happened to make her heart skip a beat whenever he was near?

"I don't know…" she said slowly. "I, uh,"

"Mandy," he said. "Look at me." She'd been looking everywhere except at him. She was trying to avoid those beautiful brown eyes. They got her every time.

"What have you got to lose? Except maybe the *spinster complex* that's been drummed into you?" He made her laugh. He often made her laugh, made her feel good.

She licked her lips. "Are you sure about this? My parents, I should warn you, can be relentless."

"I like you, Mandy," he said, reaching for his coffee. "I enjoy being with you. This pretense is not going to be any sort of hardship."

She nodded, then lifted her coffee to her lips. "As long as you're sure."

"I'm absolutely sure. I want to get to know you and your family."

Mandy nodded again but wondered if she'd survive when the pretense was over, and reality set it.

* * *

Saturday rolled around far quicker than Mandy had expected.

They'd organized that Noah should come to her house and they'd travel to her parents place together. After all, that's what a couple would do, right?

Of course it was right. She knew it was, but it just felt a little strange. It was then she realized she'd never taken a man home to meet her parents.

Ever.

That threw her, and she began to understand the reason her parents were so excited about Noah.

Which might be a problem down the track. She didn't want them to get too attached, since this was only a pretense to keep them off her back until after the Christmas party.

She chewed on her lip. Perhaps they were going too far with this charade.

Not that it was expected, but Mandy always liked to take something with her. To contribute in some way to the evening. Her offering this time was in the way of an apple pie. One of her favorites, and her father's too. He loved her pie.

She wondered if Noah had a favorite dessert. They hadn't discussed that sort of thing. When she thought about it, they knew so little of each other, but that would change over time.

If they stayed together. Which they wouldn't, since this was only pretend.

The thought pulled her up short.

She had just pulled a warm sweater over her head when she heard a knock at the door. "Come in," she called, checking herself out in the full-length mirror. "I'll only be a moment."

She leaned in and applied a perfect pink lipstick, nothing too bold, brushed her hair, and strolled into the living room.

She looked up in horror as she saw Horrible Harry standing there, confident as ever. "Nice outfit," he said, stepping toward her.

Her heartbeat sped up. It was bad enough he harassed her at work, but to come to her home? "Get out, Harry." Her hands were fisted by her side.

"You don't mean that," he said, a leer on his face. He took another step toward her.

She'd expected Noah, and stupidly assumed it was him. She was more than a little annoyed with herself. "Get out, Harry," she said again, quietly, calmly.

She had no idea how she'd managed to keep her voice calm and steady.

He took another step forward.

"Get out, Harry!" Noah bellowed at him, and Mandy had never seen him so angry. She hadn't even seen him arrive. "This is your notice. You are terminated. Report to human services at 8am Monday."

Mandy stared at Noah. His back was ramrod straight, his shoulders were squared; he was ready for a fight if needed. But knowing Noah, he would keep his temper in control, and would calm down very quickly.

Harry sneered. "I'm not at work. You can't do anything to me."

Noah pulled out his cell phone. "I'm calling the police. If you aren't gone in two seconds, they'll be here to arrest you. Take your pick – losing your job or losing your job *and* break and enter."

Harry scuffled out and shoved his way past Noah. "You're lucky it's not assault too," Noah called after him.

"Are you alright?" Noah ran to Mandy, pulling her into an embrace. She lay her head on his chest and wrapped her arms around him. Her heart rate began to slow.

"I thought it was you," she whispered. "I called out for him to come in without thinking. I didn't even consider it could be Horrible Harry."

Noah looked down at her and smiled. "Horrible Harry? Is that what you call him?"

She nodded. "Yeah, because that's what he is."

He rubbed his hands around her back in circles. She dropped her head to his chest again. It was so comforting with his hands moving over her back. Heck, just standing here like this was comforting. She didn't want to move away, but they had to leave soon.

She felt protected and loved whenever Noah was around. Her eyes opened wide. *Where did that come from?*

She dropped her hands to her sides and stepped back. "I'm okay now. Thank you." He looked down at her and frowned. "Honestly, I am," she said as she stared at his lips.

Mandy pulled her gaze away and went to the kitchen. Noah followed her. "Apple pie," she said, wrapping it in a kitchen towel.

"Yum."

She smiled for the first time since Harry had arrived. "So you do like pie? I wasn't sure."

"Mandy, I like anything you cook. So far anyway." He stepped back and laughed when she pretended to punch his arm.

"Thank you. I think." She hadn't felt this happy in a very long time. Noah was good for her, and she was certain her parents would like him.

She glanced at her watch. "Time to go. Don't want to be late on your first visit."

The family homestead wasn't far out of Winston and was only about fifteen minutes drive. The snow wasn't at all heavy tonight, so they had a good run.

Noah was amazed at the winter spectacle surrounding them. "I've never seen such a beautiful sight," he said as he continued down the long driveway to the homestead. "The snow on the tree branches – it's amazing."

"Then you've been missing out big time." She looked across at his profile and smiled.

Noah reached over and squeezed her hand, keeping his eyes on the road. "I'm so glad I came here," he said quietly. "I'm especially pleased we met. If I hadn't come…"

"Look out!"

Noah slammed on the brakes as two deer scampered across the road in front of them. "Phew. Does that happen often?"

"That you almost killed Bambi, do you mean?" She laughed, and Noah smiled. Moments ago his face was stern. Troubled. Now he was relaxed again.

Mandy put her hand to his knee. "We're almost there. Not far to go now."

He held the steering wheel tightly with both hands. "Relax. It's unlikely we'll come across more deer. Besides, we're just minutes away."

Driving a little more cautiously this time, Noah pulled in next to the homestead.

"You've got to be joking me!"

He looked across at her curiously. "Mandy?"

"See all these cars? My parents have obviously invited the whole mob." He stared at her. "To meet you no doubt." He continued to stare. "My sisters and brother and their partners? The whole gang is here." She slapped her hands to her face. "Do you want to leave?" She didn't think he'd want to stay under these circumstances.

He pulled her hands down. "Mandy," he said, getting far too close for comfort. "Why on earth would I want to leave? Besides, I hear your mom is a really good cook!"

He laughed so much she couldn't stay mad.

Suddenly the mood changed, and he cupped her cheeks with his hands. She stared into his eyes and swore she could see all the way to eternity.

"Noah," she whispered.

"Mandy," he whispered back, moments before brushing his lips across hers.

Her hands went up around his neck and she pulled him closer. "I, uh,"

She jumped at the loud tapping on the car window. It was her father. Great timing.

She sighed.

"Okay, to the lion's den we go."

* * *

Noah stepped through the door and wondered how the hell he'd ended up here. Mandy was right – this was not what he signed up for. But she was worth it.

For a moment he pondered stepping back into the cold snow-covered courtyard where his car was parked. Then he felt Mandy's hand hook through his arm and it gave him the confidence to move further into the house.

He was introduced to Mandy's family one by one, but there was no way he'd remember all those names – there were just too many of them.

Given time, things would be different.

"So young man, what are your intentions with my daughter?" Joseph Scott began to laugh once the words were out.

"Let go his hand, Father, and leave him alone." Mandy looked up at him, checking out his expression. "It's not funny."

Helena hooked her arm into Noah's free arm. "You are very handsome," she told him, staring up at him. "Mandy has done well."

Noah could barely control his laughter.

"Mother!" Mandy was as red as a beetroot.

He assured her it was okay. He was enjoying himself. He truly was.

He'd had a hunch Mandy's family were going to be a little – eccentric – but not as much as this. He liked them and felt comfortable almost immediately.

"What did you bring for your daddy, honey?" Joseph was opening up the kitchen towel to take a peak. "My favorite! Thank you, sweetheart." He leaned in and whispered. "Don't tell your mommy, but your pie is much better than hers!"

"Noah likes pie too, so you might have a fight on your hands tonight."

Her father looked him up and down. "Really? The man has good taste."

They eventually managed to get past the entrance and into the living room. It was crowded to say the least, with few chairs left to sit on.

The noise level was beyond what Noah was used to, but Joseph managed it quite easily. "Quiet down you lot. I want to hear how these two met."

He waved his hands as he bellowed above the noise, and soon it was peaceful.

"We met at work," Noah told them. "I was transferred here after Alfred Kingston had his heart attack." He turned to Mandy who sat next to him. "I think it was love at first sight. At least it was for me."

Mandy was blushing, and he lifted a hand to her cheek. He couldn't help himself. She looked so delicious, he leaned in and stole a kiss.

Everyone clapped and whistled.

"What is wrong with you people?" Mandy scolded them, then stormed out into the kitchen. Her mother followed.

"She's touchy tonight," Joseph said quietly. "Is everything alright with you two?"

Noah wondered whether to tell him about Horrible Harry but decided it was Mandy's story to tell. "Just nervous about me being here, I guess." He smiled and gazed around the room.

It was an awful lot to take in. Mandy had such a big family. He couldn't begin to contemplate what it must have been like growing up. Being an only child, his life was completely different.

His eyes landed on the decorated Christmas tree, lit up with hundreds of tiny fairy lights. "You like it?" Joseph asked.

"I've never seen one this big in a house before," he answered, distracted by everything going on around him, and watching out for Mandy's return.

Everyone was silent. It was so quiet he felt uncomfortable all of a sudden. "I've never lived where there was snow before," he suddenly said, trying to break the silence.

"Where are you from?" It was Joseph again. He was genuinely interested in him.

"Buckeye. Lived there all my life. Until now."

Joseph contemplated that for a moment. "This must be a huge change for you – going from a big city to a little town like this. What about your parents? Where do they live?"

Noah felt the color drain from his face. He was dreading this. He hadn't even told Mandy yet. "They're both dead," he said, looking down into his hands on his lap. "Car accident."

"I'm sorry, son. I shouldn't have asked." And Noah knew Joseph was genuinely sorry, but it would come out sometime.

"It's okay. Honestly." He looked up briefly and saw Mandy standing in the doorway. The shock on her face was plain to see. "Excuse me, Sir." Noah stood to go to the distraught Mandy.

He wrapped his arms around her, trying to comfort her. "I should be comforting you," she whispered so no one else could hear.

"It's alright, Mandy. Don't upset yourself." She looked up at him, tears in her eyes. "What happened? No. It's none of my business." She pushed her face into his chest. If it had been under better circumstances, he would be enjoying it.

"They died in a car accident about six months ago. It was a drunk driver." He took a deep breath. "Please don't distress yourself over this. Although it wasn't very long ago, I've learned to accept it."

"Time for dinner!" Helena's voice rang out across the room. "Everyone into the kitchen."

He felt Helena pat his back, as if to say, *you're alright. I approve*. It made him feel warm inside.

"We'll just sit in the living room for a minute if that's okay," Noah said to her, and Helena nodded. They just needed a minute to regroup. Mandy wiped at her eyes.

"I'm fine," she said. "This is an experience you won't want to miss." She grinned at him despite her tear-streaked face.

As she stood she pulled him up and toward the kitchen.

The kitchen benches were covered with a variety of foods. First courses, side dishes, and desserts. There were plates and cutlery and napkins.

The table was set for ten.

Mandy's family hovered around the food, taking bits of this and that. Noah stood back and watched in amazement. He'd never seen the likes of it before.

"Come on, or you'll miss out," she said, pulling him behind her.

Noah had never seen a family like this. And for that he was truly sorry.

* * *

Mandy tied her messy hair back into a ponytail; sometimes she hated it. Why she was the only one in the family with fluffy hair was beyond her. And it was infuriating at the same time.

Noah said he'd enjoyed meeting her family last night. She had no idea how.

It was too much. Way too much.

At first she was angry at her mother, for it would have been all her doing. She could hear her father now; *No dear, that's not what you arranged with Mandy, and it will be far too much for Noah on his first visit.*

As always, her mother would have won out. Helena could wrap her little finger around Joseph – he was putty in her hands.

It all turned out alright in the end. Little did Noah realize the Christmas party would be even bigger, with all the cousins and aunties and uncles also coming.

She covered her face with her hands. What a debacle it would be.

She sat on the side of the bed. She'd made such a mess of things. She'd dragged Noah into it all as well.

She checked her watch. He would be here any minute.

He'd insisted they have lunch today, to make up for all her upset last night. But it wasn't necessary, and she told him so.

She heard a knock at the door and peeked through the window to check it was him. She didn't want a repeat of yesterday.

As she opened the door, he leaned in and kissed her briefly on the cheek.

She wanted more.

She pulled him into the entrance and stood staring up at his lips. Those thick luscious lips that called to her.

She reached up, slowly putting her arms around his neck and pulled him down.

Their lips were only an angel's breath away before he spoke. "Are you sure this is what you want?"

She pulled back. He'd broken the spell. "Well not anymore." She turned her back to grab her scarf and coat off the rack near the door.

"I thought we'd go to one of the nearby towns and find somewhere for lunch."

She stopped what she was doing. "We could have lunch here."

"Or we could go to my place. Everything is packed away now, so it's not a huge mess anymore."

She stared at him for what seemed like ages. "I could make a picnic lunch."

He stared at her. "It's snowing," he said blandly.

"So, we'll have an inside picnic." Instead of waiting for an answer, Mandy turned toward the kitchen. "Blueberry muffins?" she called over her shoulder.

"You had me at inside picnic," he said, coming up and wrapping his arms around her. "Your place or mine?"

He leaned down and kissed the side of her neck. He'd never done that before. Not that she was complaining. It felt nice and sent warmth shooting through her body.

She reached across to the loaf of bread, pretending to ignore his advances.

"You don't like it?" She could hear the hurt in his voice.

She laid the bread on the board, ready to butter the slices. "I didn't say that, did I? It's just…"

"Just what?"

"You don't have to pretend when there's no one else around." The words were out before she could stop them. And she didn't really mean them. She felt closer to Noah every time she saw him.

He suddenly stepped away from her, and Mandy felt bereft.

She turned around to face him. His face was white and tense. "I'm sorry, Noah," she said, reaching up to cover his cheek. "I, I didn't mean it."

He grabbed her hand and pulled it down. "Not as sorry as I am."

Noah headed for the front door, grabbing his scarf and coat on his way out.

"Noah?" She was genuinely surprised at his reaction. "I'm sorry if I upset you," she said, but it made no difference. He left without another word.

* * *

He was a fool.

A total and utter fool. Why he opened his heart to another woman he'd never know. He should have learned after his break-up with Abigail.

They'd broken up more than two years ago, since then he'd protected his heart from ever being shattered again. He couldn't endure that sort of pain again.

He'd felt hollow after their split, and the feeling didn't leave him for a very long time.

He should have kept his distance with Mandy too.

The moment he laid eyes on her, he knew there was something between them. The moment they touched, he was gone.

He thought Mandy was different. He truly did.

Noah knew the 'pretend boyfriend' line was only a pretense to keep her parents happy, but somewhere along the way things became more serious.

At least it had for him. He was certain Mandy was onboard with it too, but after her cutting words, perhaps not.

She sure wasn't acting that way today.

What was wrong with him?

Abigail cheats on him, and Mandy dumps him.

She did, right? That's what happened?

He thought back to their conversation.

No, that's not what she said. But their relationship was not real to her. It sure as hell was to him.

He didn't want to be her *pretend boyfriend* any more. He wanted to be her real boyfriend.

He wanted to hold her, and not only when her parents were around. Not only when they were out in public.

He wanted to hold her wherever they were, whenever he wanted, and he especially wanted to hold her for eternity.

Somewhere along the line Noah had fallen in love with Mandy.

Chapter Five

"I think I just broke up with Noah."

Tears streaming down her face, Mandy ran into Helena's arms.

"What? No!" Helena pulled her into an embrace, and Mandy cried until there were no tears left to cry.

As they sat together in the living room, Joseph came in to find out what all the ruckus was about. "What I saw last night was not a couple about to break up," he said quietly. "You've got it all wrong."

"I agree," Helena said. "What I witnessed was a young man very much in love. And you didn't seem too unhappy either."

Mandy looked from one to the other of them. "Do you think so," she asked between sobs. "We had a fight. Today. And he walked out." Tears began to stream down her face once more. Helena handed her a box of tissues.

"Walked out?" Joseph asked. "On *my* little girl? The nerve of him!"

It wasn't his fault. Mandy knew it was all her doing. Why hadn't she kept her mouth shut?

She knew exactly what had happened. Noah was getting under her skin and she didn't like it. Didn't like it one little bit.

She'd gotten scared.

Scared that maybe things had gotten serious. Had become real.

That's not what she had planned.

Her idea was they'd pretend to be together to keep her parents off her back. When did it all go so wrong?

"Do you love him?" Helena's voice broke through her wayward thoughts. "Mandy. Do you love him? Answer me honestly, sweetheart."

Mandy nodded. She'd known it from the first day they'd met. From the moment they'd touched. She'd been lying to herself all this time and didn't even realize it.

"And you've told him, right?" Both her parents sat on the edge of their seats waiting for her to answer.

"I, uh,"

"Mandy. Did you tell him?"

She shook her head and looked down into her lap. "No." The words came out so quietly she barely heard them herself.

"Oh Mandy. Really?"

Without her permission, her tears began to stream down her face again.

"You may not know this," her mother told her quietly, "But I didn't like your father much when I first met him."

"Hang on…" Joseph interrupted.

"Shush Joseph," Helena told him. "But I loved him from the moment I saw him. Mandy, look at me, sweetheart."

Mandy looked up and stared at her mother through her tears.

"Are you willing to let him go? That's the question you have to ask yourself."

Mandy nodded knowing Helena was right. *Was she willing to let him go?*

"What I saw last night was two people who cared very much for each other." Helena patted her hand as she spoke gently. "Two people who were very much in love."

Mandy couldn't hold back. She had to tell them the truth. "I did it for you both."

Helena looked confused, along with Joseph. "Did what?"

She sniffed. "Noah was to be my pretend boyfriend." Her mother stared at her in shock. "So I could bring someone to the party," she said quickly.

Her parents both sat in silence.

"But somehow everything changed. He is so kind and caring," she wiped her nose with a tissue. "And I feel good when he's around. He even," She wasn't sure whether she should tell them this part. "He protected me when someone broke into my cottage yesterday."

Her father stood. "Someone broke into your cottage? Why didn't you tell us? Is that why…"

"Yes, that's why I was upset yesterday, but Noah made it all okay."

Her mother smiled and nodded her head. "You *are* in love with him."

"It's all too late, Mother," Mandy said. "I don't think he'll want me anymore."

* * *

Mandy arrived at work at 9am sharp.

At the very moment Harry Simpson was walking out. "You, you…" he yelled. "This is your fault. I wouldn't have lost my job except for you."

She froze momentarily, then found her voice. "No, this is your fault, Harry. Your actions caused this."

Before she knew what was happening, Harry lunged at her. He grabbed her arm and pushed her. Suddenly she was on the ground, a scuffle going on around her.

"Call the police." It was Noah's voice, calling to one of her colleagues. Two of the other male reporters pinned Harry down while Noah helped Mandy to her feet.

"And an ambulance."

Mandy brushed herself off, despite the pain in her hand. "I think I'm okay," she said with a shaky voice. It had all happened so quickly.

A chair was pushed under her, and a glass of water forced into her hand. She went to take a sip and winced.

The glass dropped to the ground.

Noah kneeled in front of her. "Where's that ambulance," he shouted.

He held her other hand. "I'm sorry Mandy," he said. "This is my fault. I should have made sure Harry was gone before you got here."

She nodded but didn't answer. She was in too much pain to think straight.

The police arrived, handcuffed Horrible Harry, then took statements from all the witnesses, while the paramedics checked Mandy out.

"Looks like a broken wrist, and possible shock too," one of the paramedics told Noah. "It requires a trip to the ER."

Mandy didn't say a word. She was dumbfounded. She'd planned to come into work today, get on with her work, and avoid Noah at all costs.

She didn't foresee anything like this happening. Not in a million years did she expect Harry to physically attack her.

"Can I ride with her?" It was Noah's voice, pushing through the fog.

"Are you a relative?"

She was shocked to hear Noah's answer. "I'm her boyfriend."

The paramedic agreed, then put a splint on her wrist. Noah help Mandy to her feet and lead her to the ambulance.

"Where's your cell phone?" he asked. "I need to ring your parents."

Mandy had to think hard. Everything was happening around her, and it was all out of her control. The fog in her brain wasn't helping one iota. "In my bag I think?"

Noah rummaged through her bag and prepared to call her parents. He wasn't sure what kind of reception he would get after yesterday's performance.

* * *

Noah waited in the cubicle in the ER.

Mandy was having an x-ray and they wouldn't let him go with her.

He admonished himself for not seeing this coming. Harry had broken into her home – he should have realized he was capable of much more.

He sat with his head in his hands. His head hurt from worry. But more, he regretted his actions yesterday and should have stayed to talk to Mandy about it.

Their charade had gone way further than a pretense. At least it had for him. In the short time he'd known Mandy, he'd come to really care for her.

His heart shattered after their argument. He should have learned from the past – you can't fix a problem without offering a solution.

He knew exactly what the solution was, but whether Mandy would agree was another thing entirely.

"Noah." Helena's voice was abrupt but also worried.

"She's having an x-ray," he said, knowing exactly why he was getting the reception he was.

"What the hell happened?" Joseph demanded. "Why didn't you protect her?"

Noah knew Joseph was right – he should have been there when Harry left, to ensure Mandy was safe. Stupidly, or perhaps naively, he hadn't thought Harry would go that far.

Not to harm someone he supposedly loved. Or at least lusted after.

"I'm sorry," he said. "It's all my fault." He put his head in his hands again, not wanting Mandy's parents to see his distress.

"Noah," Helena said, more gently this time. "I know you love our daughter, and she loves you." She walked over and touched him gently on the back. "What are you going to do about it?"

"She, she loves me?" He looked up to the older woman, his heart breaking over what had occurred.

"She certainly does. And it's as plain as the nose on your face that you love her."

He frowned. "I,"

Helena stood straight. "For goodness sake, Noah! I've seen the way you look at her, and how tender you are with her." Her glare burned him. "That's not just friendship, it's far more than that."

Noah was on his feet as Mandy was wheeled back in. "What did they say? Is it broken?"

She shook her head. "I won't know until the doctor comes around." He leaned forward and kissed her on the forehead.

"Mandy, I'm sorry. This is all my fault." He reached for her other hand and squeezed it.

"Thanks for coming," she said to her parents. Helena stepped forward and hugged Mandy gently.

"It was a shock, that's for sure."

A nurse rushed into the room and took her blood pressure and temperature. "The doctor will be here shortly," she said, then disappeared once more.

She'd only been gone a few minutes when an older man entered. "I'm Doctor Halloway," he said. "Orthopedic surgeon. I'm afraid the break is bad and requires surgery."

"Oh no!" Helena was distraught.

"Someone will come and prepare you for surgery shortly." And then he was gone.

Mandy took it in her stride. "It is what it is, Mother. Don't distress yourself. What's important is the people I love are all here to support me."

Noah stared into her eyes. He wanted Joseph and Helena to leave so he could talk to Mandy alone. But he knew that wouldn't happen and felt bad for being so selfish in Mandy's moments of need.

Instead he leaned down and brushed his lips against hers. "I love you too," he whispered, hoping the others couldn't eavesdrop on their private conversation.

Mandy glanced up at him with her beautiful blue puppy dog eyes. "You do? Why the heck didn't you tell me before?"

"Because I'm a damned fool. A stubborn idiot." He put his arms around her, careful not to bump her broken wrist.

"What is wrong with you two?" Joseph interjected roughly. "It's plain as day you two love each other. Now move aside, son, I want to hug my little girl."

Chapter Six

With her arm in plaster, Mandy was allowed to leave hospital the next day.

Noah took her to straight her parent's home. He wanted to protect her, but it wouldn't be right moving into her cottage, or her moving into his. Not in a small town like this.

The compromise was she would stay with her parents, and he would sleep there too, in the spare room.

Harry Simpson had been charged but released on bail. There was no way Noah was trusting him to stay away – not after what he did to Mandy.

He stood at the bay window, staring out across the large expanse of land the Scott's owned. The beauty before him was far beyond anything he'd seen before.

"We should cancel this year's party," Joseph said. "Given the circumstances."

Noah turned around at his words, but as an interloper, decided it was not his place to comment.

"Don't you dare, Daddy!" Mandy had just come downstairs and heard the conversation. "My broken wrist is no reason to cancel out. Tell him Noah."

He walked over to her and placed a light kiss on her forehead. "It's not my place." He put his arm around her shoulder and led her to a chair. "Cup of coffee?"

Joseph looked long and hard at Noah. "Young man," he said affectionately. "You are part of this family now. I respect your opinion."

Noah nodded, despite being taken back at the show of affection. "I say don't cancel. It's not for another week or so, and Mandy will be less fragile by then…"

"I am not fragile!"

He already knew what her response would be, but said it anyway. "Like I was saying, Mandy will be in less pain by then."

She nodded her agreement.

"Besides, I'd love to meet the rest of the family."

"It's your life, son. Don't blame me for the consequences." Joseph smiled and walked away shaking his head.

"It's not as bad as that," Mandy said, laughing. "It's like it was at the weekend, only three times as many people."

Noah groaned. "Seriously?"

"Seriously." She leaned into his shoulder. "Everyone is going to love you."

Noah put his head to the side, leaning it against Mandy's. He was exactly where he wanted to be.

"I could do with a hand in here," Helena called from the kitchen.

He looked at Mandy. "Go," she said. "I'll be fine. Mother will be grateful for your help."

"Pancakes! I haven't had pancakes for breakfast for years." Noah was near drooling with anticipation.

Helena laughed. "You have to earn your food around here. Can you set the table please, then we can all eat."

Noah stopped in his tracks. He hadn't been asked to do that in years. It was echoes of his mother.

The last time was a few days before his parents died in that horrific accident.

No! He wasn't going to think about that now. But he knew his parents would be looking down at him now. And he was certain they would approve of Mandy and her entire family.

Good choice, his mother would be saying as she nodded at him. He wished they were here to meet Mandy. They would love her for sure, and she would have loved them.

"Are you alright, Noah?" Helena's voice pushed through his thoughts.

"Yeah sure." But he wasn't. Not really. "Just thinking about my mom. She would love you all," he said, his voice breaking.

Helena walked over and hugged him, just like his mother would have done.

He loved this family. And he sure as heck loved Mandy.

Now he had to do something about it.

* * *

"Do me a favor, son?"

Joseph handed him a set of Christmas lights. "Climb up that ladder and secure these lights. I'm getting far too old for these shenanigans."

Noah started up the steps. "Besides, you're much taller than I am. You'll be able to reach from the middle of the steps." Joseph laughed as though it was a huge joke.

But it was true. He was always the tall and lanky one. At least now it was helping someone.

With the party just hours away, they were putting the finishing touches to the double garage. Most of the party would be out there, although Mandy had said it often spilled into the house. Especially with the elderly aunts.

He was nervous, to say the least. This was going to be a big affair, bigger than he'd ever attended. Except for the office Christmas parties they'd held back home.

But this one was far more important.

He wanted to meet the rest of Mandy's family, but was terrified they wouldn't like him. He'd returned to work a few days ago, after the police had deemed Harry Simpson too big a risk to Mandy and put him in jail.

As much as he wanted to spend more time with her, there were pressing things at the office he needed to attend to. Otherwise he'd be working from the homestead, which would mean the same result.

Less time spent with Mandy.

The surgeon said her arm was healing well, and despite the late blooming bruises she'd endured, she was in very little pain now.

He climbed back down the steps. "That looks perfect," he said. "Anything else?"

Noah looked at the box Joseph pointed to. "Helena has high expectations for this party. Every year we go through this rigmarole." He laughed, then added, "Get used to it, son. It's your job from now on."

"I hope so," Noah whispered, not wanting anyone else to hear. "I sure hope so."

* * *

The moment arrived and all the aunts and uncles, cousins, brothers and sisters, and a few strays rolled in to the homestead.

They all had their offering for the evening, whether that be an appetizer, main course or dessert. Some brought rolls, dips, or crisps.

No matter which way you looked at it, this family liked its food. With her arm still in plaster, Mandy hadn't baked for tonight, but looking around him, Noah was certain it wouldn't matter.

His stomach started to rumble.

"You can't possibly be hungry," Mandy scolded him. "You've done nothing but eat since you arrived here."

"And I've got the body to prove it!" He laughed and pulled Mandy closer. "You know I'm not going to remember all these people, right?"

"You will over time. Everyone here tonight is special to our family." She squeezed his hand. "That includes you," she whispered. She got up on her toes and kissed him gently on the lips.

"Whoo hoo!" One of her teenage cousins clapped and whispered.

Another, much younger one had a completely different idea. "Yuk. Really?"

"Go away, Mason," Mandy told him. "Noah, this is Mason. The family brat." She chuckled, but Mason didn't appreciate it and ran inside. "Don't mind him. One day he'll want to kiss a girl and it will be a different story," she said.

Noah leaned in and brushed her lips with his. "I can vouch for that," he said. "I remember being like Mason once. A very long time ago."

"You did a fabulous job of the decorations," Aunty Mary told him. "Joseph told me it was your handy work," she said, seeing his surprise. "Nice catch, Mandy."

He felt the heat creep up his face. "He is," Mandy said. "Oh, you're blushing," she said surprised.

"No, I'm not."

"Are too."

"Now children, stop arguing," Helena told them jokingly, bringing the chips and appetizers in to place on the large table Noah and Joseph had placed in the middle of the room.

The party was noisy but friendly, and Noah began chatting with various family members. He even remembered some of their names.

They'd just finished dessert when Joseph banged a large spoon on a pie tin. "Righto. Righto. Everyone be quiet. Just a few words if you don't mind." After a few seconds, quiet overtook the room.

"As you may have discovered by now, we have a newcomer this year. Come forward, son." He indicated Noah to move closer to where he was standing. "This is Noah Gleeson. Get used to seeing him at these parties, because he's dating my daughter!"

The room erupted into clapping and whistling. Then Joseph hushed the room again. "I believe Noah has a few words to say."

All eyes turned to him, including Mandy's. "I would like to say thank you for making me feel welcome. Mandy has a wonderful family, as I've discovered. Everyone has been so kind to me. I only have one more thing to say."

He walked over to Mandy, then dropped to his knees. He fumbled in his pocket, then pulled out a little black box. "Mandy," he said. "I love you more than words could ever express. Will you marry me?"

Everyone was shouting and clapping and whistling so much he didn't hear her answer. "Shush down everyone," Joseph said. "I didn't hear what my little girl said."

"I said yes," Mandy said between tears. "A hundred times yes!"

Noah's heart rate quickened, and his hands felt clammy. *She said yes!*

He slid the ring on her finger. Now all they had to do was set a date, not too far in the future, he hoped.

Epilogue

Mandy stood looking at herself in the full-length mirror.

She wore the same wedding dress her own mother had worn at her wedding, and her sisters had too.

It was a family tradition that she hoped to pass down to her children one day.

Helena was fussing with her veil. "It's fine, Mother. Really."

She circled her daughter doing a last-minute inspection. She nodded. "Yes, you're right," Helena said.

"Stop being so nervous," Mandy told her mother. "Everything is fine." Her plaster had only recently been removed, and her break was perfectly fused, the surgeon had told her.

Harry Simpson was tucked up in jail where he belonged, after a trial that found him guilty. How could they not with so many witnesses?

But she wasn't going to think about that today.

Her devastatingly handsome fiancée was standing in the little chapel, waiting for her to appear. No doubt as nervous as her parents.

"Last minute lipstick," Helena said. "What about the rest of you girls? Lipstick?" She waved it in the air, and Mandy's sisters laughed.

"No Mother, we're all fine," Jenny told her. She opened the door a crack. "The music has begun! It's time to go, sis."

Mandy straightened her back, and Helena pulled her veil forward. "Love you, Mandy," she said, running out the door to take her place in the chapel.

Joseph came in and hooked his arm through hers. "Ready?" he asked, looking his little girl in the eyes.

"As I'll ever be," she said. "I really love him, daddy," she said quietly.

Joseph squeezed her hand. "I know, honey. We all do."

They made their way to the front of the chapel, where he handed his daughter over to the newest member of the family.

"We are gathered here today…"

She listened as Noah said his vows with tears in his eyes. He held both her hands and squeezed them gently.

When it was her turn, Mandy said her vows, then said, "I do. I most certainly do."

"Then you may kiss your bride, Noah!"

Noah push her veil back and looked into her eyes. "I love you so much," he said quietly so only Mandy could hear, before he kissed her.

He took her hand and they practically ran outside. They were surrounded by their family and friends in no time.

Mandy felt confetti and rice slide their way down her back. "I'll get it out for you later," he promised.

"I'm sure you will," she whispered in his ear.

Noah leaned in and kissed her gently.

Joseph strolled up to them. "Welcome to the family, son," he said.

Helena wasn't far behind him. "They're looking down, watching you, Noah" she said softly. "They'd be very proud."

She leaned into him and hugged him tight. "We'll never replace your parents," she whispered. "But we'll always be here to support you."

Someone threw a whole box of confetti over them and broke the spell. "Off to the reception now, you two," Helena said.

Mandy couldn't wait to see what life with Noah would be like.

THE END

From the Author

Thank you so much for reading my book – I hope you enjoyed it.

I would greatly appreciate you leaving a review where you purchased, even if it is only a one-liner. It helps to have my books more visible!

About the Author

Multi-published, award-winning and bestselling author Cheryl Wright, former secretary, debt collector, account manager, writing coach, and shopping tour hostess, loves reading.

She writes both historical and contemporary western romance, as well as romantic suspense.

She lives in Melbourne, Australia, and is married with two adult children and has six grandchildren. When she's not writing, she can be found in her craft room making greeting cards.

Links:

Website: *http://www.cheryl-wright.com/*

Blog: *http://romance-authors.com/*

Facebook Reader Group:
https://www.facebook.com/groups/cherylwrightauthor/

Join My Newsletter:
https://cheryl-wright.com/newsletter/

www.ingramcontent.com/pod-product-compliance
Lightning Source LLC
Chambersburg PA
CBHW071543100726
47908CB00004B/1481